DISNEY's A CHRISTMAS CAROL

Produ... ...y Kapke

...d by Robert Zemeckis

DISNEP PRESS
New York

Copyright © 2009 Disney/IMD

All rights reserved. Published by Disney Press, an imprint of Disney Book Group.

No part of this book may be reproduced or transmitted in any form or by any means,
electronic or mechanical, including photocopying, recording, or by any information
storage and retrieval system, without written permission from the publisher.

For information address Disney Press, 114 Fifth Avenue, New York, New York 10011-5690.

Printed in the United States of America

First Edition

1 3 5 7 9 10 8 6 4 2

Library of Congress Catalog Card Number on file.

ISBN 978-1-4231-1794-0

For more Disney Press fun
visit www.disneybooks.com
Disney.com/ChristmasCarol

Ebenezer Scrooge was a mean old man.
He liked money more than he liked people.
When anyone wished him a merry Christmas,
he said, "Bah! Humbug!"

Scrooge owned a countinghouse. He paid his lone clerk, a man named Bob Cratchit, as little as he could.

"You'll want the day off tomorrow, I suppose?" Scrooge asked Cratchit. It was Christmas Eve.

"It's only once a year," Cratchit said.

"Be here all the earlier the next morning!" Scrooge growled.

Cratchit set off for his warm home and large family. Scrooge went to his dark, lonely mansion. But tonight his mansion was not as lonely as usual. Tonight, Scrooge's house was full—of ghosts!

The first ghost was on his door knocker. Scrooge saw the face of Jacob Marley, his old business partner. Marley had been dead for seven years!

Then, when he was upstairs in his
bedroom, Scrooge heard the front door
creak open. He heard footsteps on the
stairs. He heard the clank of chains just
beyond the bedroom door. Then a ghost
passed right through the locked door and
into the room!

"Who are you?" Scrooge asked.

"In life, I was your partner, Jacob Marrrrrleeeeeey," the ghost wailed. The chains around his body rattled loudly.

Marley was doomed to walk the earth after his death. He had been a greedy and selfish man.

"You have a chance of escaping my fate," Marley said. "You will be haunted by three spirits," Marley told him. "Without their visits, you cannot hope to shun the path I have tread."

Marley's ghost floated backward toward the window.

"Expect the first . . . when the bell tolls . . . one."

Scrooge dove into his bed. He hid under the covers. Too soon, the bell tolled a single deep, heavy note.

Scrooge's bedroom was filled with a blinding white light that came from the head of a strange creature. It looked like a child, but with white hair and the face of an old man.

"Are you the spirit whose coming was foretold to me?" Scrooge asked.

"I am!" said the child. "I am the Ghost of Christmas Past." He took Scrooge's arm with a firm grip. "Rise!"

Scrooge did. He rose off the bed. Then he and the ghost floated through the window!

The spirit and Scrooge flew out of the city. The ghost showed Scrooge a snowy road. Scrooge knew right away it was near his boyhood home.

A country wagon with a dozen boys riding in the back came down the road.

"I know them! They were schoolmates of mine!" Scrooge exclaimed.

The ghost smiled at him kindly and led him to a brick building. "This was my school," Scrooge said.

Inside, a small boy sat alone. It was Scrooge as a child. His friends had left him behind.

"Poor, poor boy," Scrooge said to the ghost. He wiped tears from his eyes.

The ghost showed Scrooge scenes from another long-ago Christmas, then another. Scrooge watched himself become greedier and greedier. He watched himself turn away Belle, the woman he once loved.

Then the Ghost of Christmas Past showed him one last scene. Belle was now a wife and mother. She had a large happy family. Scrooge felt a painful pull on his heart. That family could have been his!

"Leave me!" Scrooge cried. "Haunt me no longer!"

Scrooge found himself back in his bedroom. He tried again to hide under the covers, but something would not let him. He was pulled into his sitting room by a strange force.

The room was not the way Scrooge had left it. It was decorated for Christmas. In the middle, sitting atop a Christmas feast, was a jolly giant. He held a huge torch in his hand.

"I am the Ghost of Christmas Present," boomed the giant. "Look upon me!"

The ghost tipped his torch to the side.
A magical dust fell out onto the floor.
Instantly, the floor became like glass.
Scrooge could see right through it!

With a second dose of dust, the room began to rise. It glided out over the city. Scrooge could see the city streets through the glass floor.

Every once in a while, the ghost sprinkled dust on people below him. The dust made angry people stop fighting and hungry people less hungry.

The ghost guided the room to a small brick house. "I take it this pauper's bleak dwelling is of some significance?" Scrooge asked.

"'Tis all your loyal clerk can afford," the ghost replied.

Scrooge turned pale. This sad place was Bob Cratchit's home!

But inside, the house was warm and full of good cheer. Bob Cratchit's wife was cooking a goose. The children, laughing and making jokes, were helping her get the Christmas dinner ready.

Bob Cratchit entered the house. On his shoulder sat a frail child with a wooden crutch. This was Cratchit's youngest son, Tiny Tim.

"How did little Tim behave?" Mrs. Cratchit asked.

"Good as gold . . . and better. I believe he grows stronger and more hearty every day." But Cratchit's voice trembled. Scrooge could tell he did not believe it.

Scrooge turned to the ghost. "Spirit, tell me," he said, "will Tiny Tim . . . ?" He could not finish the thought.

"I see a vacant seat in the poor chimney corner. And a crutch without an owner," the ghost answered.

The ghost's words hit Scrooge hard. Tiny Tim could not die!

A loud cheer called Scrooge back to the scene in front of him. The children paraded in with the roasted goose.

Bob Cratchit raised his glass. "A toast," he said, "to Mr. Scrooge . . . the founder of our feast!"

Mrs. Cratchit jumped angrily to her feet. "The founder of the feast, indeed!" she ranted.

"My dear . . . Christmas day," Cratchit said in a mild voice. In a moment, she calmed down.

"A merry Christmas to us all!" Cratchit went on.

"God bless us, everyone!" Tiny Tim added.

Scrooge left the Cratchits' home feeling ashamed. The family had so little, and they still thanked him for it.

Scrooge turned back to the ghost. To his surprise, the ghost was now old. His hair was gray and his face was wrinkled.

"Are spirits' lives so short?" Scrooge asked.

"My life upon this globe is very brief. It ends tonight," the ghost told him.

When the clock next struck the hour, the ghost was gone. A new one stood in his place. It was a dark figure. A hood hid its face.

It was the Ghost of Christmas Yet to Come.

The ghost showed Scrooge scenes from Christmases in the future. He took Scrooge back to the Cratchits' house. This time the mood was sad. The Cratchits were huddled together.

"I am sure none of us shall ever forget our poor Tiny Tim," Bob Cratchit said.

Scrooge's eyes filled with tears. Poor Tiny Tim! Poor Bob Cratchit!

The next instant, the dark ghost took Scrooge to an even sadder place. It was an icy cemetery.

The ghost lifted his arm and pointed at a gravestone.

Scrooge trembled. "Are these the shadows of things that *will* be?" he asked the ghost. "Or shadows of things that *may* be?"

The ghost did not answer.

Scrooge looked at the gravestone. On it were the words EBENEZER SCROOGE.

Scrooge dropped to his knees. "I'm not the man I was," he cried out. "Why show me this if I'm past all hope?" He felt himself pulled toward the grave. It was trying to swallow him!

"Help! Spirit!" Scrooge begged. "I will honor Christmas in my heart! I will not shut out the lessons of the past . . . nor the present . . . nor the future!"

The grave drew him closer and closer. Scrooge shut his eyes.

With a start, Scrooge woke up. He was in his bedroom!

He danced around with joy. "I'm still here!" Then Scrooge ran to the window and threw it open. He spotted a boy on the street below. "What's today, my fine fellow?" he called.

"Today?" the boy said. "Why, Christmas day!"

Scrooge's heart swelled at the boy's words. It was Christmas! He hadn't missed it after all!

Scrooge asked the boy to go to the corner store for him. It had a prized turkey for sale. Scrooge could think of no family that would enjoy it more than the Cratchits. "It's twice the size of Tiny Tim," he said with glee.

Scrooge spent the day making up for every Christmas he had wasted. He gave money to the poor and a smile to everyone he met. It was a very merry Christmas indeed.

The next morning, Bob Cratchit came to the countinghouse.

"A full sixteen minutes late," Scrooge chuckled to himself. He put on a stern face. "I am not going to stand for this sort of thing any longer!" he growled at Cratchit.

Cratchit looked like he was going to faint.

"And therefore . . ." Scrooge's frown changed into a huge grin. "I'm about to raise your salary!" Scrooge clapped Cratchit on the back. "I'll do whatever I can to help your family," Scrooge added.

Day after day and month after month,
Scrooge kept his promises.

And to Tiny Tim, who got well, Scrooge
was like a second father.

The ghosts had taught Scrooge well. Never
again would he let wealth or selfishness cloud
his heart.

He was a changed man.